PUFFIN BOOKS

SUPERPOWERS
THE JAWS OF DOOM

2 ⁵⁰

Books by Alex Cliff
SUPERPOWERS series

SUPER
THE JAWS OF DOOM
POWERS

ALEX CLIFF

ILLUSTRATED BY LEO HARTASS

PUFFIN

PUFFIN BOOKS

Published by the Penguin Group
Penguin Books Ltd, 80 Strand, London WC2R ORL, England
Penguin Group (USA) Inc., 375 Hudson Street, New York, New York 10014, USA
Penguin Group (Canada), 90 Eglinton Avenue East, Suite 700, Toronto, Ontario, Canada M4P 2Y3
(a division of Pearson Penguin Canada Inc.)
Penguin Ireland, 25 St Stephen's Green, Dublin 2, Ireland (a division of Penguin Books Ltd)
Penguin Group (Australia), 250 Camberwell Road, Camberwell, Victoria 3124, Australia
(a division of Pearson Australia Group Pty Ltd)
Penguin Books India Pvt Ltd, 11 Community Centre, Panchsheel Park,
New Delhi – 110 017, India
Penguin Group (NZ), 67 Apollo Drive, Rosedale, North Shore 0632, New Zealand
(a division of Pearson New Zealand Ltd)
Penguin Books (South Africa) (Pty) Ltd, 24 Sturdee Avenue, Rosebank,
Johannesburg 2196, South Africa

Penguin Books Ltd, Registered Offices: 80 Strand, London WC2R ORL, England

puffinbooks.com

Published 2007

3

Text copyright © Alex Cliff, 2007
Illustrations copyright © Leo Hartass, 2007
All rights reserved

The moral right of the author and illustrator has been asserted

Set in Bembo
Typeset by Palimpsest Book Production Limited, Grangemouth, Stirlingshire
Made and printed in England by Clays Ltd, St Ives plc

British Library Cataloguing in Publication Data
A CIP catalogue record for this book is available from the British Library

ISBN: 978-0-141-32133-2

To the real Max Hayward and Finlay Yates,
true superheroes . . .

CONTENTS

JUST IMAGINE . . .

a ruined castle with crumbling grey
stone walls and a moat of deep, dark
water. Across the moat an overgrown
grassy track heads down the hill, over a
stream and into a dense wood of old,
gnarled trees. High above the castle's
one remaining tower, a hawk is circling
in the air. It has spotted something. Two
eight-year-old boys, carrying bags and

spades, are walking through the trees towards the castle. They don't know it yet, but what happens today will change their lives forever. The hawk hovers, its black eyes fixed on the two boys. Their adventure is about to begin . . .

CHAPTER ONE

THE HAND IN THE WALL

Max Hayward shifted his bag on his back and passed the heavy spade he was carrying into his other hand. He wished he could just chuck it down on the grass and leave it. But he couldn't. He and his best friend, Finlay, were going to the castle to search for its hidden dungeon that day. If they found the dungeon, they'd probably need spades

3

to clear undergrowth and earth away.
To take his mind off his aching arms,
Max looked at Finlay. 'Did you watch
Gladiator Challenge on TV last night,
then?'

'Course,' replied Finlay. *Gladiator
Challenge* was their favourite

programme. Contestants got to do all sorts of challenges.

'Wish I could be one of the gladiators,' said Max.

'I'd like to be in charge like the Emperor,' Finlay said. 'It'd be wicked.'

Dumping his bag on the ground, he jumped on to an overturned bath that was rusting outside the rickety shed they were passing.

'Let the challenge begin!' Finlay roared, holding up his spade like a staff as he pretended to be the Emperor, the man who set the gladiators their challenges.

Max laughed at him. Finlay was always messing around.

Finlay waved the spade in the air and felt really cool but then his feet slipped on the wet surface of the bath. 'Whoaa!' he cried, his arms whizzing round as he crashed down into the long wet grass.

Max grinned. 'Don't think the Emperor's got much to worry about!'

Finlay sat up. There were bits of wet grass sticking to his thick blonde hair. Seeing Max still grinning, he said, 'But you're the one standing in a cowpat!'

As Max looked down in surprise Finlay leapt to his feet and grabbed him in a headlock. 'Sucker! I was just joking!'

'Oi!' Max shouted but his protests were muffled in Finlay's jumper. However, Max was the taller of the two boys and his arms were longer. Reaching across Finlay's body, Max grabbed Finlay's leg and threw his own weight forward at the same time. The

two of them crashed to the ground.
They rolled apart and jumped to their
feet. Max's brown hair was now covered
in wet grass too and his jeans were
damp. There was a dark splodge of
something that looked like mud on his

knee. He prodded it and pulled a face. 'Yuck! It smells like poo.'

Finlay burst out laughing as Max wiped his jeans clean with a handful of wet grass. 'Quits?' he asked.

Max grinned. 'Come on, let's go to the castle.'

They picked up their spades and bags again.

Hardly anyone ever went to the ruined castle on the edge of their village because the path to it was so overgrown, but for the last month Max and Finlay had been hanging out there. It was cool. Max's dad, who was into history and stuff, had told them it had been built eight hundred years ago on the site of an ancient Roman temple.

'There's nothing to see of the temple

now,' he had said, 'but thousands of years ago Romans made sacrifices to the great goddess Juno there. They were very scared of Juno because, long ago, she had almost destroyed the great hero Hercules. The Romans feared that if she turned her powers against them they wouldn't stand a chance.'

Max and Finlay weren't that interested in Roman temples and ancient Roman goddesses but they did like to play at being gladiators in the castle and searching for the hidden dungeon. No one nagged them to do things when they were at the castle and they had even made a den in the one tower that was still standing.

'Look, some stones have fallen down,' Max pointed out as they reached the stone and wood bridge that led across the moat.

Finlay frowned. 'It must have been the storm last night. Did you hear all that rain and thunder?'

Max nodded. 'It woke me up. I hope the tower's OK. It might have been hit by lightning.'

The boys hurried across the bridge. The rays of the early sun had not yet reached the gatehouse and it was cold and shadowy inside its walls. Stumbling across the stones on the floor, Max and Finlay climbed out of an arch that had once been the doorway and into the inner keep.

The keep was a large area of grass encircled by the castle's crumbling outer walls. Opposite the gatehouse was the

tower the boys used for their den.
Quite a few broken stones lay around it
but it was still standing.

'It looks OK,' Finlay said in relief.
'Let's check our stuff.'

Dropping their spades by the
gatehouse the two boys ran across the
grass. As they stepped inside the tower
they saw that several more stones had
fallen out of the walls and were lying
on the floor.

Finlay went over to one of the lowest
windows. It had a thick ledge where he
and Max kept some stuff – an old
blanket, some comics and sticks they
had collected to use as swords.

'Look at those new holes in the walls,'
Max pointed out. 'They must be where
those stones fell out from.'

'This is a deep one.' Finlay looked at a hole opposite the doorway. He put his hand into it. It felt cold and he could feel gritty dust and sand beneath his fingers. He reached in further,

wondering how far it went. 'It goes back really far. Look!' His arm was almost in the wall up to his elbow now.

He grinned. 'It's the hole of doom,' he said, pushing his arm right up to his shoulder inside it and wriggling his fingers. 'Help! Help!' He pretended to struggle as if the wall was pulling him into it. 'It's got me, Max! I can't escape! You've got to help me! Help . . .'

Suddenly something inside the wall grabbed his hand.

'Arghhh!' Finlay yelled in shock. He tried to yank his hand back, but whatever was holding it held on fast. 'MAX!!'

Max grinned and headed for the door. 'Stop messing about, Fin. Let's go outside.'

'I . . . but . . . I . . .' Finlay gasped, wild-eyed, almost breaking his arm in his struggle to get away. But he couldn't escape. Fingers with sharp nails seemed to tighten around his knuckles. 'Max! I'm not messing!' he yelled frantically. 'Something's got my hand.'

Max sighed. 'Fin . . .' he began but suddenly he saw the look of sheer panic in Finlay's eyes and the grin dropped from his face. 'What? You mean for real? Something's really got you? But it's just a wall!'

'So why's it hanging on to me, then?' Finlay shouted in desperation.

Max grabbed Finlay's free hand and pulled. At just that moment the sun rose above the tower and chased the shadows on the gatehouse wall away.

Max pulled with every last bit of his strength.

Finlay felt the grip on his hand loosen. With a surprised yell, he and Max fell back into a heap on the ground.

'Are you OK?' Max demanded. He looked at the wall where Finlay had been. The stones above the hole were crumbling.

'Fin! The wall!' he gasped. The boys scrambled to their feet.

For a moment, they couldn't believe what they were seeing. The stones above the hole dissolved into dust, leaving a rectangular opening. Deep inside it, a dark shape slowly began to form.

'W-what is-s th-that?' Finlay

stammered, pointing in horror at the opening.

A grey, withered face stared straight out at them.

CHAPTER TWO

DANGER!

The boys stared at the face in the wall. It was a man's face. His eyes were open but he didn't move.

Max began to back away, shaking his head. 'Oh no, this is not good.'

Dust had caught in the wrinkles of the man's face. His hair was thin and straggly and his left cheek had a long scar across it.

17

'Is it . . . is *he* . . . dead?' Finlay whispered.

'He's stuck in a wall, Finlay!' Max hissed. 'Of course he's dead!'

Suddenly the man blinked.

'Arghh!' Max and Finlay both yelled. They turned to run.

'Wait!' a voice snapped out. It was a voice that sounded strong and used to being obeyed. Both Finlay and Max stopped and slowly turned round.

The man blinked, clearing dust from his eyes. 'I am sorry,' he said, his voice becoming gentler. 'Do not be afraid. I mean you no harm.'

Max and Finlay stood with their backs pressed against the archway. The man looked down on them. His golden-brown eyes were large and

heavy lidded, almost like a lion's. Finlay
gulped. 'Who . . . who are you?'

The man's answer stunned them.
'Hercules,' he replied.

'Hercules!' Max echoed. 'Like the
superhero?'

'Not *like* the superhero,' the man said,

pride flashing across his face. 'I *am* the superhero. I am Hercules!'

'He's a loony!' Finlay whispered to Max.

'Let's get out of here,' muttered Max. 'OK then, Hercules,' he said loudly. 'We'll just be going now.' He took a step towards the door.

'Wait! I really *am* Hercules!' the man exclaimed. 'I completed twelve labours in my youth and have spent thousands of years secretly protecting mankind.'

'Yeah, right,' Max muttered to Finlay. But Finlay had paused.

'Look how old he is, Max. He can't be a real person.' Finlay's eyes widened as he had an idea. 'Maybe he's a . . .'

'No, I'm not a ghost,' the man replied, seeming to read Finlay's thoughts.

'Touch my face and you'll see.' A glint
of amusement lit up his eyes as he saw
the boys' alarm at the idea. 'Go on. I
will not bite you.'

Finlay and Max looked at each other.

'You go,' Max said, pushing Finlay
forward.

Finlay approached the man cautiously. He climbed on to the window ledge and slowly reached across and touched the man's cheek. His skin was as wrinkly as a thousand-year-old alien's but it felt warm. Finlay pulled his hand back sharply. 'He's not a ghost, Max!' he said, jumping to the ground again. 'I don't know what he is, but he isn't a ghost.'

'I told you,' the man said, looking down at them. 'I am Hercules.'

The two boys exchanged glances. He couldn't be, could he?

Max edged closer. 'If you *are* Hercules, what are you doing here?'

'I have been imprisoned by the goddess Juno,' Hercules replied, a look of anger darkening his face. 'This castle was built on the site of one of her ancient temples. She lured me here last night by threatening to unleash her fury using thunder and lightning, on that village through the trees . . .'

'That's where we live!' Finlay exclaimed.

'Juno knew I could not stand by and watch innocent people be harmed,' Hercules went on. 'I came to stop her. We battled and in a moment of weakness I let myself be distracted. Juno seized her advantage. She used magic to take my powers and imprison me in the walls of this tower.'

'Why?' Max asked, still suspicious.

'She hates me,' Hercules replied. 'She always has. My father, Jupiter, who is the king of the gods, was married to her but then he met my mother, an ordinary human, and fell in love. For thousands of years Juno has been pursuing me. Now she has finally succeeded. She has captured me and taken all my powers.'

'So you're not a superhero any more,' Finlay said. 'Your powers have really gone?'

'Gone?' echoed Hercules. 'No, they have not gone.' He looked straight past them. 'They are there – in the gatehouse wall!'

Max and Finlay swung round. The sun had risen above the tower and was now shining on the archway of the ruined gatehouse. Around the archway were eight flat stones. In each stone, apart from one, a bright symbol was glowing. There was a hammer, a pair of wings, an arrow, a shield, a tree with an acorn, a leaping stag and a lion.

'My seven superpowers,' Hercules said softly. 'Strength, speed, agility, defence, size-shifting, accuracy and courage. Juno has placed them in those seven stones. Without them I will grow older and older until I wither away to dust.' He looked longingly at the gatehouse. 'If I could just touch the symbols all my powers would flow back into me. But I cannot get to them. To torture me, Juno has decided to make the stones in front of my face crumble every morning just as the sun hits the gatehouse wall. I can look out from here and see my powers but I cannot reach them. After twenty minutes the symbols on the wall will fade, the stones will close again and I will be shut up in the darkness until the next day.'

Max stared. There was a bit of his mind that was saying this can't be

happening. But the glowing symbols on the gatehouse wall were real enough, and as he looked into the tall man's golden eyes he felt his doubts slip away. 'Can we do anything to help?' he asked.

Hercules threw back his head and laughed but it was in a kindly way. 'You boys? Help me? No. I called you back when you were running away because I did not wish you to be frightened by me, but you are just ordinary mortals and you cannot help. I must face my fate. My own weakness betrayed me. It is right I should suffer now.'

'But there must be something . . .' Max broke off. 'What would happen if *we* touched the symbols?' he asked suddenly. 'Would the powers come out of the stone and into us?'

'Yes,' Hercules replied. 'The powers will pass into anyone who touches the symbols.'

'So could we bring the powers back and give them to you?' Finlay said, getting excited.

'You must not even think such a thing!' Hercules said in alarm. 'It is far too dangerous. I have only ever seen gods and heroes carry superpowers before. I do not know what would happen if an ordinary mortal were to try and take them. The power might be too much for the human body to bear.'

'You mean we might explode or something?' Max asked.

'Or die?' said Finlay.

'Truthfully, I do not know,' answered Hercules. He looked from one boy to the other. 'Listen to me; it is very brave of you both to offer to help. Very brave indeed. But this is my battle and I cannot – *will not* – let you endanger yourselves.'

Max and Finlay exchanged looks. They knew they were thinking the same thing. 'We can do it. We want to help you,' Max told Hercules determinedly.

'Yeah, you can't let this Juno win,'

Finlay put in. 'If we get the powers for you, you'll be able to break free and go and fight her.' He swung round. 'Come on, Max. Let's do it!'

'Wait!' Hercules burst out as Finlay ran to the entrance of the tower. 'This is madness!'

Excitement — as well as a dash of fear — flashed through Max. He couldn't help thinking of Hercules' words. *It is far too dangerous.* His heart pounded as he went to the door and looked at the symbols. 'Maybe . . . maybe just one power first, Fin,' he whispered.

'OK, but how do we decide who tries to get it?' Finlay asked.

'Let's toss for it,' said Max, pulling out a ten-pence piece from his pocket. 'You call.'

'Heads!' Finlay called out as the silver coin spun high into the air.

Max caught it and put it down on the back of his hand.

'Well?' Finlay asked excitedly.

'You look, Fin,' said Max, slowly uncovering the coin for his friend to see.

A mixture of disappointment and relief flooded into Finlay's eyes. 'It's heads,' he said, looking at Max. 'You're going.'

CHAPTER THREE

JUNO

Max's legs felt suddenly shaky. So *he* was going to be the one to touch the stone. 'OK,' he said slowly, looking at the symbols glowing on the gatehouse.

'Wait!' Hercules commanded from inside the tower.

But Max felt there was no way he could back out now. 'So I just put my

hand on the symbol,' he muttered to
Finlay. He forced a smile. 'Easy.'

'Good luck,' Finlay said anxiously.

Max took a deep breath and headed
out of the entrance. The walk across the
keep towards the gatehouse seemed to
go on forever. He could feel Finlay
watching him, hear the crunch of every
stalk of grass under his trainers, hear
Hercules' muffled protests.

It's going to be OK, he told himself, as
a hawk cried out overhead. *It's going to
be easy. Just pick up the power . . .*

He imagined how the power might
destroy him. Maybe he would explode
– his head bouncing round the grass,
his body splattered against the gatehouse
walls.

He forced the picture away.

Almost there.

The hammer symbol glowed on the wall directly in front of him. *Strength*, he thought. The hammer holds the power of strength. He stopped in front of it. It looked as if it was traced on the wall

with white fire. *When he touched those lines, would it be hot like fire? Would it burn him?*

Gritting his teeth, Max lifted his hand and brought it down firmly on the hammer.

Heat scorched into his fingers. He almost pulled his hand away but forced himself not to move. The stream of warmth flowed into his arm and through his body all the way to his toes.

'Whoaa,' Max muttered under his breath. His skin began to tingle all over.

After a few moments the stone under his fingers went cold and the hammer symbol faded away.

Max cautiously took his hand off the wall. His body felt light but also strangely heavy at the same time. Stars seemed to be dancing in the corners of his eyes. But at least there'd been no explosion.

Result, thought Max in relief.

He looked down. His spade was lying on the ground. *What would happen if . . .?*

He couldn't resist it. Max picked up the spade. It felt as light as if it were a toy. Holding one end of the metal shaft in each hand he brought his hands together. The metal bent in two as easily as if it had been a cardboard tube from a roll of wrapping paper.

'Cool!' Max breathed.

Swinging round he saw that Finlay was standing anxiously by the doorway of the tower.

'It's OK!' Max yelled in excitement.
He started to run across the keep. 'I'm
all right and it's worked and . . .'

CRASH!

A clap of thunder boomed through
the air and Max heard Hercules cry
out. A jagged fork of blazing lightning
shot down out of the sky. Max

instinctively shut his eyes against the bright light. When he opened them, he stared.

A woman was now standing between him and the tower. But she wasn't an ordinary woman. She was much taller than a normal person and her dark eyes flashed with black fire. She wore a flowing white dress and a cloak of brown-grey feathers that swirled about her. Her long brown hair was caught up on top of her head. She looked beautiful but very dangerous. Looking down at Max, she laughed.

Baddie! The alarm bells shrieked in Max's brain. He was about to make a run for the tower back to Finlay and Hercules when he realized something.

He was strong. He could bend metal with his bare hands.

Throwing back his shoulders he started to march towards the woman instead. He could deal with *her*!

The woman clicked her fingers. Max stopped in mid-stride. He couldn't move a single muscle from the neck down.

'Max!' Finlay shouted in alarm. He started to run towards the woman. 'What have you done to him?' he yelled.

Glancing at Finlay as if he were an irritating fly, the woman clicked her fingers again. The next second, Finlay had frozen too. 'Hey!' he gasped. But the woman just laughed evilly and then trained her eyes, like death lasers, on the tower.

'So the once-great Hercules now has to rely on children to help him,' the woman called scornfully, her ancient voice echoing like a thunderclap. 'Did you honestly believe you could escape from me so easily? How *could* you think I would let you get your powers back in such a way, Hercules?'

Max could see Hercules' face in the stone wall. He roared like a caged tiger. 'Juno! This is . . .'

But Juno the goddess cut across him. 'You should have known that a mere human could not possibly help you.' She turned to sneer at Max. 'Particularly not such a pathetic little worm.'

Finlay gave an angry shout. 'That's my friend you're talking ab–'

Juno waved her hand and Finlay's

voice was silenced. He tried to open his mouth, but Juno's magic held it shut. He struggled desperately, but could only gasp out a few muffled sounds.

Juno turned back to Hercules. 'Only true heroes can carry the powers of the gods, Hercules. You know that.'

'And who's to say this boy isn't a hero?' Hercules demanded.

'What, him?' said Juno, laughing incredulously at Max.

'Yes, him!' Hercules roared. 'It took great courage to collect that power – it was the act of a true hero.'

Juno laughed scornfully. 'It takes more than one act to become a hero. You had to complete twelve labours before the world was foolish enough to recognize *you* as a hero, Hercules.' Her eyes looked contemptuous. 'That maggot of a boy wouldn't be able to complete even *one* of your tasks – even with the superhuman strength he now possesses.'

Max was getting fed up with being called a worm and a maggot. 'I bet I could!' he shouted.

Hercules and Juno both looked at him.

'Me too!' Finlay managed to gasp out despite Juno's magic.

A slow smile spread across the goddess's face. 'Really? So you two think you could complete one of the tasks that Hercules once did – that you could drive away a flock of man-eating birds maybe or fight a sabre-toothed Nemean lion or even slay a nine-headed monster?'

'Yes!' Max shouted.

'Prove it,' Juno challenged.

'How can we?' Max exclaimed. 'There aren't such things as monsters and man-eating birds now. But if there were, we'd fight them, wouldn't we, Fin?'

Finlay nodded eagerly.

A look of amusement lit up Juno's eyes, rather like the look of a cat with a mouse to play with – and kill.

'Well, well,' she said softly. 'I can see this could be rather fun.'

'No!' Hercules commanded. 'You must not, Juno. They're just boys. They . . .'

Ignoring him, the goddess swung round to look at Max. 'One sabre-toothed lion coming up!' She clapped her hands. There was a flash of lightning. Three wood pigeons that had been roosting in the walls flew up into the air in alarm.

Max tensed in shock, half-expecting to see a lion jumping out of the ruins towards him. But nothing happened.

'Juno!' Hercules yelled in horror. 'What are you doing?'

The goddess smiled gleefully. 'They wanted a lion, so now they've got one.' Her eyes glittered at Max. 'It'll be in the woods. Probably heading towards the village. Nemean lions have always been fond of human flesh. Do you have any friends or family living in the village?'

'Y—yes,' Max cried, desperately trying to free himself from Juno's magic that still held him fast.

'You'd better catch it quickly, then,' Juno said. 'You wouldn't want them to come to any harm. You know, I think I'm going to enjoy this.' She clicked her fingers and suddenly both boys found they could move again. 'And just

to stop my fun being over too quickly,
I'll give you a chance,' she went on.
'You can keep the power of
superhuman strength you picked up
just now. If you capture the lion, then
the power will return to Hercules. If
you don't capture the lion, the power

will leave you and be lost to the world forever. Still, you two probably won't care about that.' She laughed delightedly. 'You'll be too busy being the lion's lunch.'

'Juno, you cannot do this!' Hercules shouted, pounding the wall. 'Let me fight it instead! They are just boys!'

'And I thought you said they were heroes.' Juno's eyebrows lifted. 'Soon we'll find out which of us is right.' She raised her hands and then paused in mid-clap. 'Oh, and, Hercules, your time today is almost up.' She glanced at the sun. 'Just two more minutes before the stones go back into place.' Her eyes flashed mockingly. 'You will see nothing, Hercules, but I hope you enjoy imagining what is to come!'

The goddess clapped her hands together and vanished in a flash of lightning.

For a moment neither Fin nor Max moved.

'So we're going to fight a lion,' Max said slowly. 'A man-eating, sabre-toothed lion.'

'Yes,' Finlay gulped. 'Can I just say one thing?'

'What?' said Max.

'Help!' exclaimed Finlay.

CHAPTER FOUR

INTO THE WOODS

'Juno!' Hercules bellowed, his voice ringing out around the castle keep. But the only sound that came back was the faint cry of a hawk overhead.

Max thought about his new super-strength. 'It'll be OK.'

'OK!' Finlay exclaimed. 'Have you gone mental, Max? There's a Nemy-wotsit lion in those woods, and *we've* got to capture it before it eats anyone!'

'But I'm super-strong,' Max told him. 'Look!' He picked up a stone and, holding it high, he squeezed hard. The stone crumbled as easily as if it had been a lump of dry soil.

'Wicked,' Finlay breathed.

'If you think *that's* wicked, watch this!' Max said, his eyes falling on a huge boulder that was lying near the base of the tower. It was about the size of a table. Marching over to it, Max lifted it into the air. 'Hi . . . yah!' he exclaimed, holding it above his head. Then just for good effect he took one hand away and waved at Finlay. He had never felt so cool. 'Bet I can throw this really far!'

'No, boy! Wait!' Hercules called quickly. 'You don't know your own strength . . .'

But it was too late. Max was already chucking the boulder across the keep.

The moment it left his hands, Max realized it was a mistake. He'd thought the boulder would land a few metres away, but propelled by his superhuman strength it shot through the air like a turbo-charged rocket.

'It's going to hit the gatehouse tower!' Finlay gasped in alarm.

He and Max watched in horrified fascination as the boulder sailed towards the gatehouse roof.

'Quick, Max! Get inside!' Finlay yelled. Grabbing Max's arm, he yanked him backwards into the tower.

He was just in time.

With a huge crash the boulder smacked into the top of the gatehouse. Hundreds of stones exploded into the air. They crashed into the walls and came raining down on to the grass like grey cannonballs. The boulder fell into the moat on the other side of the gatehouse. There was a huge splash and a riot of indignant squawking from the ducks.

Sheltering in the tower from the chaos around them, Max and Finlay exchanged looks.

'Whoops,' Max said shakily. He looked at the ragged top of the gatehouse wall, now several metres shorter than it had been. 'Guess I shouldn't have done that.'

There was a groan from behind them. Hercules had his head bowed.

'Are you all right, Hercules?' Finlay asked him cautiously.

'Arghh!' Hercules roared, thumping

the walls of his prison. 'A Nemean lion is roaming free. Two foolish schoolboys are the only adversaries to stand in its way.' His voice sank to a despairing whisper. 'So many people's lives will be lost.'

Max didn't like being called foolish but he guessed Hercules had a point.

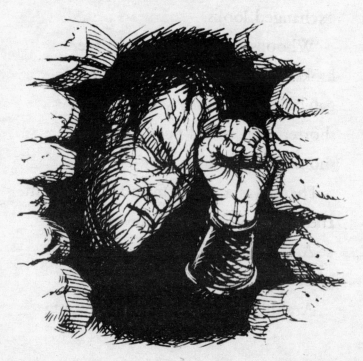

Chucking the boulder probably wasn't the cleverest thing he'd ever done.

'I'm sorry about the gatehouse,' he said awkwardly. 'But we will stop the lion, won't we, Finlay?'

Finlay nodded. 'Yeah. With Max's mega strength it'll be easy.'

'Easy!' Hercules exclaimed. 'The Nemean Lion is a monster whose only desire is to kill. His strength is immense. His teeth are legendary. He will rip you to . . .'

But before he could finish his sentence there was a grinding, crunching noise. The boys gasped as the stones around Hercules' face suddenly re-formed and they found themselves simply staring at a blank grey wall.

'He's gone!' Finlay exclaimed.

Max looked round. The glowing symbols in the gatehouse wall had vanished too. 'It's part of Juno's spell,' he remembered. 'Hercules can only see out for twenty minutes.'

'So, now we're on our own,' Finlay said slowly.

Max nodded. 'With a sabre-toothed lion to capture in the woods.'

'Um, Max . . . what do you think Hercules was about to say?' Finlay said cautiously. 'You know, the "he will rip you to . . ." bit he was in the middle of when the wall came back?'

Max looked nervously in the direction of the woods. 'I guess we're about to find out!'

★

Taking the spades as weapons, the two boys crossed the moat and headed down the track towards the woods.

'I wish we had some more weapons,' Finlay said, looking at the bent spade he was carrying.

'A bazooka would be good,' Max gulped. The trees were looming up in front of them and the closer they got the more nervous he felt.

As they reached the woods they passed an old crumbling building that had once been part of the castle stables.

'Do you reckon there might be anything we could use in here?' Finlay said hopefully. They peered inside, but the building was empty apart from some sacks and a heap of old rope in a corner. 'We could take the rope,' Finlay said. 'It might be useful, I guess.'

Max swung the coil of rope easily on to his shoulder. 'So what are we going to do?'

Finlay was always the best at coming up with brilliant ideas. He thought for a moment. 'OK,' he said at last. 'How about you use your super-strength to wrestle the lion to the ground, then I hit it on the head with one of the spades to knock it out, then we bring it back to the castle.'

Max hesitated. He'd have preferred a plan that involved them finding a get-lost tranquillizer gun and giant net but he guessed it was the best they were going to come up with. 'OK,' he agreed.

Exchanging nervous looks they headed into the trees.

The forest track led up a steep hill. Usually there were all sorts of sounds in the woods – birds calling, rustles in the undergrowth, but today there was no sound at all.

'It's really quiet in here,' Finlay said.

'Yeah,' Max agreed. 'It's like all the birds and animals have gone.'

Finlay swallowed. 'Probably run away from this lion.'

'Or been eaten,' Max added. He could feel his hands sweating. What were they going to find?

They stopped at the brow of the hill.

Below them the woods stretched down into a clearing far below. Leaves and branches were scattered across the ground of the clearing and bushes on either side looked as if they had been heavily trampled.

'It was probably just the storm last night,' Finlay said, trying to sound brave. 'It . . .'

A long, low growl rumbled through the clearing below.

'Um, Finlay,' Max whispered slowly. 'Did you hear that?'

Finlay gulped. 'Yep.'

The growl rose in volume. The leaves on the bushes in the clearing began to tremble.

'Maybe we should go and think up some more ideas,' Finlay said, taking a hasty step backwards.

'Good idea,' Max agreed. 'Come on, let's . . .'

But before he could finish, with a roar like an erupting volcano, an enormous golden lion sprang out of the bushes into the clearing below.

The boys both gasped.

This was no ordinary lion. It was as

big as a rhinoceros and had a jet-black ruff of hair around its enormous head. Two enormous dirty-yellow fangs hung down out of its mouth and its eyes gleamed red.

The beast flicked its tail and looked up the hill. Its vicious eyes fell on the boys.

'It's seen us!' Finlay gasped.

The lion roared savagely.

'Max!' cried Finlay. 'I've got a new idea!'

'Me too!' exclaimed Max. He turned. '*Run!*'

CHAPTER FIVE

LIONS DON'T CLIMB TREES!

Max and Finlay charged back down the path the way they'd come.

I should stop. The thought hammered through Max's head. *I've got superhuman strength. I should stop and fight it.*

Glancing over his shoulder he saw the mighty lion burst over the brow of the hill behind them. Suddenly, fighting it seemed like quite possibly the dumbest idea he'd ever had in his life.

'It's going to catch us!' he shouted as the lion caught sight of them again and bounded forward. Max chucked away

the rope, so he could run faster. It catapulted through the air, flying down the hill.

If only I could run as quickly, Max thought desperately.

Beside him, Finlay's breath was coming in short gasps. 'Quick!' he panted.

Looking behind him again, Max saw that the lion was gaining on them with every second. 'What are we going to do, Finlay?' he yelled.

'Climb a tree!' Finlay shouted back. 'Lions don't climb trees!'

Sprinting to the nearest tree, Max began pulling himself up. It was easy with his super-strength. He swung himself up easily through the branches.

Finlay followed him more slowly.

Twigs scratched his face and tore at his
hair. A sharp branch scraped down
his cheek. He could feel blood start to
trickle down his face but he ignored it.
'We're out of its reach!' he gasped to
Max mid-climb as the beast reached the
base of the tree and snarled up at them.

But the boys didn't stop until they
were more than halfway up. Then they
looked down. The lion was slashing
savagely at the trunk with claws that
looked like curved black blades.

Max's breath was short in his throat.
This lion was real! It wasn't some
creature in a horror film who could be
made to disappear by turning off the
TV. He could see the hairs on its back
and smell its stinking breath that reeked
of rotten meat. It looked up at him. Its

fangs glistened, razor sharp and horribly real. Max clung on to the tree with shaking hands and legs. What would those teeth do to him or Finlay if they fell out of the tree?

At least we're safe up here, he thought.

The lion sank back on its haunches. Hope leapt through Max. Perhaps it was going to give up and prowl away. *Then we can get down*, he thought, *and maybe go and find some proper weapons and . . .*

Suddenly the lion stood up on to his hind legs and grabbed the tree trunk with its knife-like claws.

'Wh—what's it doing?' Finlay stammered.

The lion's strong muscles tensed and he jumped from the ground. The next minute, he was inching his way up the tree, his belly flat against the rough bark, his long claws digging into the wood.

'I thought you said lions didn't climb trees, Fin!' Max exclaimed in panic.

'Someone must have forgotten to tell that to *this* lion!' Finlay gasped.

Max looked round desperately, but there were no trees near enough that they could climb or jump on to. The lion moved another enormous paw towards them, sinking its claws into the bark half a metre further up the tree. It hauled its heavy body up slowly.

'What are we going to do?' Max shouted to Finlay.

Finlay thought for a second. 'We can either stop and fight or keep going up.'

They looked at each other. 'Keep going up!' they gasped together.

They began hauling themselves up one branch at a time until they reached a part of the tree where they had to stop because there was a big gap before the next branch above them.

Max stretched out. He could just

reach it. Wrapping his fingers round the wood he used his super-strength to pull himself up. He climbed up two branches more and looked down.

His heart somersaulted and he flung both arms round the trunk desperately as he realized quite how far away the ground was. The bushes beneath him looked tiny. If they fell now the lion would be the least of their problems.

'I can't get hold of the branch!' Finlay exclaimed from below. He was still at the big gap. His fingertips only just touched the branch above him. He couldn't get a proper grip on the wood. 'I can't do it!'

'You've got to, Fin!' Max shouted as he saw the lion claw itself further up the trunk towards him. Its mighty paw reached up towards the branch Finlay was standing on. 'Come on!' Max yelled desperately.

Holding on tight, he started to shin back down the tree to help. Snarling viciously, the lion swiped at Finlay's legs. Finlay yelled in alarm and jumped for the branch above. His hands just about closed round the wood. For a moment, he swung in the air, his legs kicking wildly as he hung on by his fingertips. 'Max! Help, I'm slipping!' he cried. One of his trainers came off.

Max tried to grab him, but he was too far away. Below Finlay, the lion snapped at the trainer as it fell towards him.

Max tried to lean further down the tree but he was too late. Just as the lion

spat the trainer out, Finlay lost his grip.
With a yell, he fell through the air,
arms and legs windmilling wildly.

Max watched in horror as Finlay just
missed the lion's turned head, crashing

instead on to its neck. Finlay's hands instinctively closed around its thick mane and he jolted to a stop. The lion roared in fury as Finlay hung from its mane, dangling in the air above the forest floor.

'Help!' he yelled.

The lion's claws scrabbled at the tree trunk, but Finlay had caught him by surprise. As he lifted one front paw to strike the boy at his neck, the other one lost its grip. With a roar of shock the lion and Finlay fell from the tree together. They crashed down through the branches and landed on the ground in a tangle of legs and fur.

'Fin!' Max shouted.

There was a horrible moment when neither the lion nor Finlay moved. But

then Finlay rolled groggily off the lion's
back and on to the ground. He
staggered to his feet, rubbing his head.

'I'm OK!' he called to Max.

'Run, Finlay! Run!' Max yelled from
the tree as he saw the lion twitch. He
swung himself down the gap in the
branches.

The lion snarled savagely and started to get to its feet.

'All right, maybe I'm not OK!' Finlay gasped.

Fixing its red eyes on him, the Nemean Lion crouched low and prepared to spring . . .

CHAPTER SIX

FIGHTING BACK

Finlay's heart banged in his chest as he stared up at the lion. Its fangs were dripping with drool and its eyes burned hungrily. How could they ever have imagined they would catch a lion like this? The lion's muscles bunched as it got ready to pounce.

'No!' he heard Max yell.

Breaking off an enormous branch

from the tree, Max chucked it as hard
as he could at the lion. The lion gave a
surprised yowl as it smacked into its
back.

'Get lost!' Max shouted, and Finlay
looked round to see him half-scrambling,
half-falling down the tree in his hurry
to come and save him.

'Don't be stupid, Max!' Finlay yelled.
'Stay in the tree!'

But Max ignored him. Tearing off
another huge branch on his way down
he chucked it even harder at the lion. It
smacked into the lion's ear. 'Leave my
mate alone!' he shouted as he jumped
down to the ground.

The beast roared indignantly.

Max saw his chance and while the
lion was busy roaring he picked up the

branch from the ground. Swinging it round like a club he tried to hit the lion with it. But this time the lion was ready. It grabbed the bough in its massive jaws. With one easy movement it bit through it.

'Run, Max!' Finlay yelled.

Max desperately wanted to but he knew that if he did the lion would turn its attention back to Finlay.

Spitting splinters out of its mouth the lion lowered its massive shoulders into a hunting position and stalked slowly forwards. Empty-handed, Max backed away, his heart pounding as he stared into the lion's eyes.

His back collided with the tree trunk behind him.

I'm strong, he reminded himself over

the frantic beating of his heart. *I can fight, even with just my bare hands.* He remembered how easily he had thrown the boulder at the castle. He could wrestle the lion to the ground.

Trying to remember everything he

had ever seen on *Gladiator Challenge* about wrestling, Max gulped and threw himself right over the lion's jaws and on to its back. Grabbing its mane, he attempted to pull it down.

The lion shook its head furiously.

'Argh!' Max yelled as he smacked into the floor with two handfuls of mane in his fists. Before he had time to think whether he was hurt or not the lion twisted round and swiped an enormous paw at him.

Max dived out of the way just in time. Fear surged through him but now with the fear there was also excitement. He was super-strong. He could fight this lion!

'Hey, Max!' Finlay called from behind the lion. 'I've had an idea!'

As the lion glanced at Fin, Max saw his chance. 'Not now, Fin!' he shouted as he leapt for the lion's back again.

Wrapping his hands round its thick neck, he hung on. He'd had an idea too. He began to crush his super-strong arms around the lion's neck. The lion opened its mouth and struggled to draw breath. For a moment it fell to its knees but within a second was up again, shaking its head.

If only I get my arms right round its throat, Max thought. He tried to reach forward to get one arm under its jaw but the lion's sabre teeth came slashing down. Max pulled back but not in time to stop one of the teeth catching his right hand. He gasped in pain as blood spurted out of the jagged cut.

'Are you OK?' Finlay shouted in alarm.

But Max was too busy to answer. Trying to ignore the pain and to be thankful that it was only his hand that had got slashed and not his whole arm,

he hung on to the lion, blood running down the beast's black mane.

If only I had some rope to keep the lion's mouth shut so it can't bite me, he thought desperately.

Finlay shouted something, but just then the lion roared and Max couldn't hear what Finlay was saying above the noise ringing in his ears. Hanging on desperately, Max crushed his arms round the lion's neck as hard as he could. Out of the corner of his eye, he caught sight of Finlay turning and starting to run away down the path.

'Fin!' Max exclaimed in horror. 'Where are you going?'

But Finlay didn't stop.

The lion whipped its head from side to side. Max gasped as his hands slipped.

With a roar the lion threw itself swiftly to one side. Max lost his grip, flew through the air and thumped to the ground.

He felt as if all the breath had been knocked out of him. Gasping for air, he just managed to scramble to his feet.

His hand was oozing blood and his jeans were torn from scrambling down the tree. He looked round desperately. Where was Finlay?

He'd gone. It was just him and the Nemean Lion. He was on his own.

I'm going to die, Max thought despairingly, as the enraged beast faced him. *I'm really going to die!*

CHAPTER SEVEN

THE ROPE

Max gulped as the lion prepared to pounce. He had never felt more alone in his life.

'Hey, stinky breath!'

Max swung round. Finlay was charging back up the hill, his arms clutching the rope that he had thrown away. The lion angrily looked round to see what the new noise was too.

'Yes, you!' Finlay shouted to it as he ran up to join Max. 'Ever thought about visiting a dentist?'

'You've come back!' Max exclaimed.

Finlay stared at him in surprise. 'You thought I wouldn't?' The lion snarled.

Finlay quickly thrust the rope into Max's hands. 'Here. We can tie his mouth shut with it to stop him biting. Only problem is . . .' he exclaimed as the lion roared in fury. 'I'm not sure how we can do it!'

Max felt a sudden surge of energy now. He wasn't on his own after all. Finlay was with him! 'I know!' he gasped, ignoring the pain in his bleeding hand. 'Hang on tight to one end of the rope and get ready to jump when I say!'

The lion pounced.

'Now!' Max yelled, thrusting one end of the rope to Finlay.

To Max's relief, Finlay didn't stop to question what they were doing. He and Max dived forward together, pulling the

rope straight into the lion's open jaws.
Grabbing the lion's mane, Max swung
himself easily on to its back again.

'Here, Fin!' he shouted. 'Chuck me
your end of the rope!'

Finlay threw it as far as he could.
Max caught it and pulled both ends of
the rope with all his super-strength.

The lion began to roar in confusion
as the rope pulled back tightly against
the corners of its mouth.

Now! Max thought to himself.
Reaching forward, he threw one end of
the rope around its jaws.

The lion broke off in mid-roar as its
jaws were pulled shut by the rope. Max
quickly tied the rope tightly behind the
lion's ears.

The lion struggled in rage but its

mouth was held shut. It lashed out with its dagger-like claws.

'Quick, Max!' Finlay yelled. 'I'll tie its legs!'

Max threw the end of the rope to Finlay. Ducking and dodging to avoid

the lion's slashing claws, Finlay ran round, looping the rope around the lion's paws, then he chucked it back to Max. Max pulled the rope tightly, tying the lion's legs together. The lion grunted in surprise and collapsed on the ground.

'That's it!' Max gasped in relief, scrambling off the lion's back.

The lion struggled against the ropes, but Max's knots were too tight and he couldn't break free. It was tied up and powerless.

'You did it, Max!' Finlay exclaimed. 'You captured the Nemean Lion!'

'*We* did it,' Max said in delight. 'It was a brilliant idea to get the rope.'

Finlay grinned. 'Just call me a genius.' He frowned as he remembered something. 'You didn't really think I'd run off and wasn't coming back, did you, Max?'

Max looked at Finlay's scratched face and shook his head as he realized that deep down he'd always known that Finlay wouldn't desert him. 'No. I knew you'd come back.'

'There's no way I'd have left you to fight this thing on your own,' Finlay said. 'After all, I knew you'd need me and my good ideas.'

Max raised his eyebrows. 'What? You mean good ideas like climbing a tree?'

Finlay punched his arm. 'I didn't hear you coming up with much else at the time!'

Max was just about to punch him back when Finlay jumped away. 'Hey, stop!' he shouted in alarm.

Max caught himself just in time. 'Sorry,' he said sheepishly as he remembered his super-strength.

'Is your hand OK?' Finlay asked, seeing the blood on the back of Max's hand.

Max nodded. 'It's just a cut.' Looking at the wound he noticed something. 'Weird. Look.' He held his hand out for Finlay to see. 'It looks a bit like a hammer.'

'Yeah,' Finlay agreed. 'Cool!'

Behind them, the lion growled.

The boys forgot the unusual shape of the wound. 'I guess we should get the lion back to the castle,' Max said, turning to look at the tied-up beast.

Finlay frowned. 'Exactly *how* are we going to do that?'

'I thought you were the one who's supposed to have the good ideas!' Max grinned. 'We'll get it back like this, of course!'

In one swift movement he turned the lion upside down and lifted it high

above his head as easily as if it had
been a kitten. It snarled horribly but its
savage jaws were held safely shut by the
rope.

'Cool!' Finlay jogged alongside Max.
'You OK up there, ickle kitty cat?'

A growl rumbled out of the lion's
throat.

Finlay grinned at it. 'Eat my shorts!'

Even with super-strength it was still
hard work carrying a struggling
Nemean lion all the way up the hill
from the woods to the castle and Max
was very relieved when they finally
reached the castle moat.

'Wonder what we do with it now,' he
panted as they walked over the bridge.
'My arms are killing!'

As they reached the gatehouse the

lion suddenly began to struggle more
than ever. 'Hey! Hold still!' Max told it,
tightening his grip.

The lion yowled through its ropes
and tried to scrabble with its tied feet.

Max stumbled across the rubble. All

he could think about was getting into the castle keep and putting the beast down.

Crash!

As Max stepped out of the shadows on to the grass, there was a loud clap of thunder and a blinding flash of white light.

Max felt the weight in his arms disappear. 'Where's the lion gone?' he gasped.

'Don't worry about that. Look what's arrived!' Finlay gulped.

Standing in the middle of the castle keep was the tall figure of the goddess Juno.

CHAPTER EIGHT

LET THE CHALLENGE BEGIN!

Juno's feathered cape swept to the floor and her black eyes seemed to pierce through Max and Finlay like lasers. 'So,' she said, her gaze sweeping from one to the other, 'you have completed your task.'

Max and Finlay shrank back against the gatehouse, the rough stones digging into their backs.

'Um, yes,' Max stammered. 'We . . . er . . . we got the lion. Though,' he looked at his empty arms, 'I don't actually know where it's gone.'

Juno waved a dismissive hand. 'It has returned to the Land of the Gods. Its role here is over.' She swept closer to them. Finlay and Max pressed themselves as hard as they could against the wall as she paused in front of them.

'You surprised me,' she said, sounding almost disappointed. 'You achieved the task. Though,' she added, looking down her nose at them, 'it was by luck, not skill and courage, of course.'

'It wasn't just luck!' Finlay protested. 'Max was really brave —'

'So were you!' Max interrupted.

Juno shot them an icy glare. 'Silence!'

They hastily shut up.

'By luck,' Juno repeated and this time neither of them argued. 'Still, you completed the task and therefore,' she sighed as if bored, 'I suppose I *must* keep my side of the bargain too.'

Turning swiftly she clapped her hands and strode back across the castle keep. There was a rumbling sound and suddenly the stones began to fall from Hercules' tower.

'Hercules!' gasped Max as Hercules' worn and weathered face appeared in the stone wall.

Hercules' golden eyes lit up with relief as he saw them. 'Boys!' he exclaimed. 'You are all right.'

'We did the task!' Finlay shouted. 'We got the lion!'

'And so I will return your power of strength, Hercules,' Juno said with an irritated toss of her head.

Hercules turned angrily to her. 'You should never have risked two boys. You –'

'Enough,' Juno interrupted. 'Here. Take your power back!'

Max gasped as he felt a warm swirling feeling in his chest. It was an amazing feeling of power and strength, and then suddenly Juno clicked her fingers and all the warmth seemed to rush out of him. A golden light flashed across the keep straight from Max to Hercules. Hercules cried out and blinked as the golden light hit him.

For a moment there was silence and then Hercules slowly opened his eyes.

'His face,' breathed Finlay. 'Look, Max!'

Max stared. The wrinkles on Hercules' face were fading and his skin seemed to be losing some of its dusty grey deadness. He stared at Juno. His golden eyes seemed brighter.

'My strength. I have my strength back,' he whispered and the boys could hear the delight in his voice.

Juno laughed mockingly. 'Much good may it do you. You're still my prisoner, Hercules. It will take more than mere physical strength to break free of my magic bonds.' She pointed at the gatehouse wall above the boys' heads. 'Your other powers are still mine and so they will stay unless you regain them by the end of the week.'

Finlay and Max swung round. Above their heads six symbols were now glowing in the stone – a pair of wings, an arrow, a shield, a tree with an acorn, a leaping stag and a lion. 'You have a

week, Hercules,' Juno declared. 'And
then the rest of your powers will be
gone forever!'

Glancing back across the courtyard
Max saw a look of utter despair cross
Hercules' noble face. 'We'll help you,

Hercules!' The words burst from him. 'We'll come back in the morning and carry the rest of your powers to you!'

Juno turned on him. 'Haven't you learnt your lesson by now, you maggot? I told you only true heroes can pick up the powers.'

'But we *are* heroes,' Max protested. 'We proved it. We captured the Nemean Lion!'

'One success means nothing,' Juno sneered. 'Hercules had to complete twelve tasks before he was declared a hero.'

'We'll do more things then!' Finlay exclaimed.

'Yeah, if it'll help Hercules!' Max said.

A slow, dangerous smile spread across Juno's face. 'Oh, well, if you wish to provide me with amusement then who am I to stop you? I suppose you may try and prove yourselves heroes if you *really* want to.'

'No!' Hercules shouted.

Juno clicked her fingers and although Hercules continued to mouth protests, no sound left his lips. Juno spoke to the boys. 'So, you want to help Hercules?'

'Yes,' Max replied stoutly and Finlay nodded in agreement.

'Then every day for the next six days I will set you a task to complete,' she declared. 'A task that will be similar to one of the labours Hercules once performed. If you get here as the sun first falls on the gatehouse wall you will be able to choose one of Hercules' superpowers to take and help you for the day. If you complete the task successfully *on your own*, then that power will return to Hercules; if you fail then the power will disappear at sunset and will be lost to Hercules forever. Oh, and you'll probably have died in trying.' Her eyes glittered. 'How does that sound?'

Finlay and Max looked at each other. The dying part didn't sound good but they'd said they'd help Hercules.

'What sort of things will we have to do?' Finlay asked cautiously.

'Oh, I think maybe for starters you could kill the Nine-Headed River Monster,' Juno replied.

Max and Finlay gulped.

Juno laughed. 'So, are you still so keen to be heroes now?'

They didn't say anything.

'Oh, Hercules,' Juno said, shooting a mocking look at the tower. 'I think your heroes are changing their minds . . .'

'We're not!' Finlay exclaimed.

'No!' Max cried.

'So, it's a deal?' Juno asked, her eyes lighting up.

'It's a deal!' Max and Finlay shouted together.

Out of the corner of his eye Max saw Hercules thump the tower in dismay.

Laughing in delight, Juno clapped her hands. 'This is going to be so much fun!' She clicked her fingers. Hercules' voice came back.

'Juno! No!' he shouted. 'You cannot do this! They are just boys —'

'It's too late, Hercules,' Juno interrupted triumphantly. 'They have agreed. We have made a deal.'

'Let me go in their place. Let –'

'No!' Juno clapped her hands again and with a grinding, crunching noise the stones in front of his face began to re-form.

'Come in the morning,' he shouted. 'I will give you advice. I will –' But then the last stone moved into place and his voice was abruptly cut off.

'So,' Juno said, swinging round to Max and Finlay. 'Here are your tasks. One a day for the next six days.' She counted the tasks on her fingers. 'One – kill the Nine-Headed River Monster; two – clean the impossibly dirty stables; three – capture a giant boar; four – steal the three golden apples of the gods; five – drive away a flock of man-eating birds and finally, six,' she laughed, 'if you get that far which I very much doubt – herd twenty raging bulls.'

'And if we do them all Hercules gets all his powers back?' Max said.

Juno laughed. '*If* you do them all, which I very much doubt.'

'And we have one superpower a day to help us,' Finlay said, trying to get it straight.

Juno nodded. 'You may choose one a day. Much good may it do you.' Throwing her head back she crowed with gleeful laughter. 'Enjoy being heroes – I will have fun watching you die!'

She clapped her hands. There was a flash of lightning.

The boys blinked. When they looked again she had gone and the only reminder of her was a single brown-grey feather fluttering through the air.

For a long moment neither Finlay nor Max spoke.

Finlay broke the silence. 'Let the challenge begin,' he whispered.

Max shot him a sideways look. He knew what Finlay was thinking – this was just like *Gladiator Challenge* but for real. 'Yes,' he said, but his voice shook.

Their eyes met.

'We'll be OK,' Max said, desperately wanting to believe it.

'Yeah. All we've got to do is fight a nine-headed monster to help save a superhero's powers.' Finlay grinned and shrugged. 'What's the big deal?'

Max couldn't help but grin back. 'A Nemean lion today, a nine-headed monster tomorrow – no problem,' he agreed.

'Ah, but don't forget cleaning horse

poo out of stables!' Finlay said. 'Gross!'

'I'd rather fight the monster,' Max said
with feeling.

Finlay ran to the middle of the keep
and punched the air. 'Bring on that
monster!' he shouted.

Max raced after him. 'Yeah! We'll be
ready for it!'

They stopped in the middle of the keep and looked up to the sky. 'Let the challenge begin!' they yelled bravely.

High overhead, a hawk called out a mocking reply.

ABOUT THE AUTHOR

ALEX CLIFF LIVES IN A VILLAGE IN LEICESTERSHIRE, NEXT DOOR TO FIN AND JUST DOWN THE ROAD FROM MAX, BUT UNFORTUNATELY THERE IS NO CASTLE ON THE OUTSKIRTS OF THE VILLAGE. ALEX'S HOME IS FILLED WITH TWO CHILDREN AND TWO LARGE AND VERY SLOBBERY PET MONSTERS.

WILL MAX AND FIN SAVE HERCULES IN TIME?

WHAT HAPPENS WHEN THEY COME UP AGAINST A GIANT NINE-HEADED MONSTER?

FIND OUT IN . . .

SUPER
THE HEADS OF HORROR
POWERS

ALEX CLIFF

DID YOU KNOW?

Hercules lived in Ancient Greece. He was the son of a woman named Alcmene and the god Zeus. When Hercules was a baby he could fight snakes with his bare hands! The labours he had to complete were originally set for him by his cousin Eurystheus, King of Mycenae.

THE NEMEAN LION

This was a creature that roamed the hills around the city of Nemea and terrorized its people. Hercules tried to shoot it with arrows but they bounced off harmlessly. Instead, he had to wrestle the monster. He wore the lion's skin when he returned it to Eurystheus; the king was so scared that he hid in a bronze jar.

puffin.co.uk

YOUR
SUPER POWERS
QUEST

YOU NEED:
2 players
2 counters
1 dice
and nerves of steel!

YOU MUST:
Collect all **seven** superpowers
and save Hercules, who has
been trapped in the castle by
the evil goddess, Juno. All you
have to do is roll the dice and
follow the steps on the books
– try not to land on Juno's rock
or one of the monsters!

JOIN THE QUEST!
COLLECT ALL **7** BOOKS AND PLAY THE SUPERPOWERS GAME

① You need a **SUPERPOWER** to save Hercules, off you go!

② You've got today's power – strength! **MOVE FORWARD THREE ROCKS**

⑦ **YOWSERS!** You've left the hammer behind. MISS A GO

START

③ **OH NO!** You've landed on Juno's rock. Back to the start!

⑥ **RUN FASTER!** It's getting closer. **ROLL AGAIN**

⑧ **GO!** You're only six powers from saving Hercules. GO TO THE NEXT QUEST!

④ **EEK!** Time is running out, but you can't move until you roll a three.

⑤ **YIKES!** You must brave the Jaws of Doom. RUN ACROSS TWO ROCKS

PUFFIN
puffinbooks.com

U.K. £3.99
CAN. $0.00

ISBN 978-0-141-32133-2

YOU CAN:
PLAY BOOK BY BOOK
The game is only complete when all seven books in the series are lined
up. But if you don't have them all yet, you can still complete the quests!
Whoever lands on the 'GO' rock first is the winner of that particular quest.

PLAY THE WHOLE GAME
Whoever collects all seven superpowers and is first to land on the final
rock has completed the entire quest and saved Hercules!

REMEMBER:
If you land on a 'Back to the Start' symbol, don't worry – you don't have
to go all the way back to book one – just back to the start of the game
on the book you are playing.

GOOD LUCK, SUPERHEROES!

puffin.co.uk